Gus, Lisa & Family,

Have fun and enjoy
these short stories.
Smile & Shine for Jesus.

V. Antony, Jr. Alaharasa

11-18-01

Tales from the Heart

— The Art of Living for Young and Old —

By

V. Antony J. Alaharasan

Illustrations by

Sherry L. Fissel

Ambassador Books, Inc.
Worcester • Massachusetts

ISBN: 1-929039-09-3
Library of Congress Catalog Card Number: 2001093537

Published in the United States by Ambassador Books, Inc.
71 Elm Street, Worcester, Massachusetts 01609
(800) 577-0909

Printed in Korea.

For current information about all titles from Ambassador Books, visit our website at:
www.ambassadorbooks.com

Dedication

In fond memory of
Corinne K. Brown,
who was a dear friend
and like a mother to me.

Table of Contents

— Trust, Faith, and Works —

Blessings in Disguise. 15
Pot of Milk. 17
Run Praying 19
Darkness Hates the Light 20
Truth is More Valuable than Gold 21
Never to Yield 21
The Boatman's Long Lost Brother. 22
The Courage of Mahatma Gandhi 25
Teach My Monkey to Speak. 26

— Love and Happiness —

Gandhi's Love for All 31
The Unconditional Love of Mothers. 33
Brotherly Love 34
The Most Precious 35
The Bridge over Divisions 36
The Sage and the Sinner. 37
Butterflies and Happiness 38
Unselfish Love 39
Rain and Red Soil. 40
Happy Man without a Shirt 41
Nothing Greater. 43
Peacocks and Celebrities. 44

— Wisdom and Humility —

Humility is the Way to God 47
Two Brothers and a Priest. 48
The Heron's Revenge 49
Honeybee and Taxes. 50
Blessed Are the Humble 51
True Wisdom: Nothing Exceeds Everything. 52
Lord! All I Have Written Is Straw! 54
The Fool and the King's Staff. 55
The Elephant and the Pig. 56
Gray Hair: A Sign to Prepare for the Next Life. 57

— Responsibility and Respect —

Crossing with the Cross 61
You Could Have Hissed 63
The Empire and the Nail 64
At My Side 65
Your Freedom Ends Where My Nose Begins 67
Fool's Gold 68
The Rich Man and His Walking Stick 69
The Monkey and the Crocodile 71
Hunger for Harmony 73
The Monk and the Monkey 75
Frog or Bee Mentality 76

— Spirit of Charity, Compassion, and Kindness —

The King and the Hawk 79
Gandhi and His Shoes 80
The Truck Driver and the Priest 81
The Life Giving Tree 82
The Chieftain's Love for a Creeper 84
The Worshipping Hands 85
The Beggar's Divine Comedy 87
The Nature of a True Friend 88
Pigs Don't Pray 88
Know Your Origins 89
The Monk and the Scorpion 90
The Puppy and the Barnyard Animals 91
A Question of Possession 93
The Chieftain and the Honeybees 94

— God's Presence —

The Boy and His Kite 97
First Snow 99
A Gentle Slap 100
The Treasure Is in You 101
The Pumpkin and the Acorn 102
St. Francis and the Crabs 103
God in All Things 104
Hippy or Happy 105
The Hand Print of God 106
Unaware of God's Omniscience 107

Forward

From earliest times story telling has occupied a central place in basic human experience. Long before humans developed writing, stories communicated collective and individual memories, providing the first source of what we today would call history. But even in these early times, story telling also provided much needed entertainment. Beyond that, stories were also used to teach—as a means of encouragement or correction, and as a vehicle to transmit a sense of human values and ethics.

Even after the development of writing, oral traditions and stories almost always preceded their codification in written form. A prime example would be the four Gospels which, once written, represented the authentic oral tradition and belief of the very early Church. In secular literature, one could cite the examples of the great epic poems which always began as oral stories which were only later set in writing, often centuries after the story was first told. France's epic poem *The Song of Roland* (*La Chanson de Roland*) provides a prime example. This epic poem began as an orally transmitted story about a battle, and the story was repeated and elaborated for hundreds of years before it was first transcribed. *The Song of Roland* transmits elements of French history, provides an entertaining and engrossing story, while also teaching. It communicates a series of ethical positions and values revered by the French at that time.

Jesus Himself used stories or parables to teach, and in ancient Greece, Aesop used the entertaining, and often funny, stories of his fables to offer moral instruction. Most stories which offer psychological insight into human conduct or which provide moral instruction are also entertaining, even at times amusing. They follow the dictum of the ancient Roman poet Horace who wrote: *Omne tolit punctum gui miscuit utile et dulce.* (That person wins everyone's vote who mixes the useful with the sweet).

Father Antony Alaharasan is a natural and talented storyteller. From his childhood he had an ear for good stories, a deep appreciation of them, and a good memory to retain them. In this collection, Father Alaharasan shares with us some of the finest stories he has remembered —stories which he himself has told. They come from many sources and traditions, many of them Eastern. In his own preface Father Antony tells us that he has created some of the stories himself, while others he remembers from childhood in his native Sri Lanka. Other stories he has drawn from a wide variety of sources, both Western and Eastern.

Father Antony Alaharasan is a widely published author of eleven books, who has written extensively on Scripture and on Eastern literature, traditions, and religions. He holds a Doctorate in comparative religion from Madras University, India. Father Antony has studied at Harvard University Divinity School and has taught at Jaffna University, Sri Lanka, at Felician College, New Jersey, and at Holy Apostles College and Seminary in Connecticut. Widely traveled throughout the world, Father Antony is fascinated by cultural diversity and the comparative study of peoples and cultures.

In addition to these academic and scholarly pursuits, Father Alaharasan has served in a wide variety of pastoral positions and assignments in the Catholic Church, starting in Sri Lanka and Malaysia, as well as for the Archdiocese of New York, the Diocese of Brooklyn, and of Norwich, Connecticut. He is currently Pastor of St. Thomas More Church, North Stonington, Connecticut.

Given Father Alaharasan's richly diverse background, in terms of travel, scholarship, as well as educational and pastoral experience, it should not surprise us that these *Tales from the Heart* have the capacity both to entertain us and to enlighten our minds. Approaching these stories as readers, we might well recall the admonition announced to the congregation in some Churches of the Eastern Rite just before a reading of the Sacred Scripture: "Wisdom! Let us be attentive!"

Francis J. Greene, Ph.D.
Professor and Chairman,
Department of Foreign Languages and Fine Arts
St. Francis College, New York

Introduction

Tales from the Heart is indeed a book from the heart. These stories were treasured and stored up in my heart over the years, from my childhood until now. What Jesus said is true of me. "Every Student of the Scriptures who becomes a disciple in the kingdom of heaven is like someone who brings out new and old treasures from the storeroom." [Matthew 9:52]

During my sabbatical, my friend, Father James J. Fedigan, S.J. made arrangements for me to stay at Campion Renewal Center Weston with Jesuit friends for over a month. He said to me, "Father Antony! You are a storyteller. Why don't you write stories?"

So I locked myself up in room number 429 and I began to dig into my heart for old and new stories. I was amazed that I was able to come up with almost one hundred stories. Some of the stories like *The Monkey and the Crocodile* I learned when I was in the third grade. *The Beggar's Divine Comedy* from Rabidranath Tagore (the title is mine), which I learned in the seminary more than thirty years ago, stories from Sri Rama Krishna, and some of the stories which I read and heard from books and people and especially from Tamil Literature have remained deep in my heart. Over the years I have forgotten the sources and the authors names, except for a few. The seminal thoughts of the stories remained in my heart. So I gave my own forms, names, expressions and titles. Some of them I even composed. Some of my personal experiences are here in the form of stories, like *First Snow* and *Butterflies and Happiness.*

After every story I draw out a moral lesson.

How did the book come to be published? When I was at Campion Center, in the dining room, most of the time I sat with a saintly and scholarly priest by the name of Father Fred A. Harkins, S.J. I told him that I was working on my book *Tales from the Heart* and that I was looking for a good publisher. He said "Don't worry, I have a good friend, by the name of Gerard Goggins. I have known him for the last forty years. He is the publisher of Ambassador Books in Worcester and he has published my book *Father Fred and the Twelve Steps.*"

Father Fred is a man of action. At once he invited me to his room and called Gerard Goggins and put me in contact with Gerry. Gerry was very gracious and told me to send the manuscript. "I'll do the best I can," he said.

I am very grateful to Father Fred and to Gerry, for helping me to publish this book. May Jesus bless their generous hearts. I am also grateful for the fathers of Campion Center for the quiet and peaceful atmosphere they provided for me to write this book. I am also grateful to Ambassador Books, Inc. for bringing out this book.

I wish also to express my gratitude for my dear friend Professor Francis J. Green, Ph.D., chairman of the Department of Foreign Languages and Fine Arts, St. Francis College, New York, for the wonderful forward to my book; to Sherry L. Fissel for the beautiful illustrations; and to Michael Belz who took my photograph for the book cover.

My foremost thanks goes to my Risen Lord Jesus Christ, the GREATEST STORY TELLER who ever lived. May He fire everyone who reads this book with imagination, passion, and inspiration.

Smile and shine for Jesus.

V. Antony J. Alaharasan

Trust, Faith, and Works

Blessings in Disguise

A long time ago in India, there was a king who lived in a palace. A minister, who worked for the king, also lived there. The minister was a very positive person who always saw the bright side of life. No matter what happened in the palace, the minister would say, "Oh! This is good! Everything will be fine." Such was his philosophy of life.

One summer evening, the king was enjoying a sweet mango. While slicing a piece, the king cut off one of his fingers.

The minister, who was standing near the king, exclaimed, "Oh! This is good! Everything will be fine!"

The king was so annoyed by the minister's remark that he ordered the minister to be thrown into jail.

Now this king took great pleasure in hunting wild animals. One day he decided to go hunting in the forest.

Unbeknownst to the king, there were robbers in the forest on this very day. The robbers believed that there were gods who were angry with them, and so they were seeking to sacrifice a person of royal blood in order to appease the gods' anger. The robbers came upon the king and were delighted at their good fortune; they captured him and held him as a prisoner, eagerly anticipating the upcoming sacrifice.

In preparation for the sacrifice, the robbers gave the king a ritual bath. While bathing the king, they noticed that the king was missing a finger from his hand. Because of this defect, the robbers deemed him unsuitable for the sacrifice. So, the robbers released the king and sent him home.

The king was very happy indeed! He rushed to the palace, ran to the jail, and freed his long-time minister.

The king embraced his minister and said, "Oh! This is good! Everything is fine! It is good that I lost my finger. You were right my friend! What I thought was a tragedy turned out to be a great good. Losing my finger saved my life! May you in your wisdom find the grace to forgive me for my rash error!"

> *When times of trial come, we must trust in God. We must have faith that good will come from what seems to be bad. For we cannot see the final outcome of the trial— only Jesus can. Blessings are often disguised as tragedies, and God can bring good from events that first seem to be terrible. St. Paul tells us, "All things work together for good to those who love God."[Romans 8:28]*

Pot of Milk

In Hindu legend, there is a messenger of God—like an angel—called Narada. One day, God and Narada looked down from heaven at a farmer going about his daily tasks.

"Did you see my servant, the farmer, today?" God asked Narada. "Despite all the work he had to do in the fields, he did not fail to invoke my name many times during the day."

"That is nothing," Narada answered. "I can do much better than he. I can invoke your holy name millions of times a day in spite of my work."

So God gave Narada a test. He told Narada to go down to Earth and to get a big pot of milk. Then God told Narada to balance the pot of milk on his head while circling the entire Earth without spilling a drop.

Narada did as he was told. He went to Earth from the heavenly quarters and carried the pot of milk on his head while he circled the globe. At the end of the day, Narada appeared before God.

"I circled the entire earth with the pot of milk on my head, and I did not spill a drop," Narada told God.

"Yes," God replied, "but how many times did you invoke my name today?"

"One time," Narada replied hesitantly.

"But my servant the farmer invoked my name more than one hundred times while he worked in the fields today," God said.

Narada protested to God, "But I had to balance the pot of milk on my head and circle the whole earth without spilling a bit of milk on the ground."

"Yes," God said, "but common folks, like my servant the farmer, never cease to invoke my name many times a day despite their daily problems and duties."

> *Sometimes we can be so busy serving God that we lose our perspective and pay more attention to what we are doing than to whom we are serving. Humility is required to keep the focus on God rather than on ourselves.*

Run Praying

Lal Bahadur Shastri, the Prime Minister of India, had constant advice for his sons: "Be honest and hard working. Hard work is equal to prayer."

As Rabindranath Tagore, the Indian poet and Nobel Prize winner, would say, "God is there, where the tiller is tilling the hard ground and where the path-maker is breaking stones. He is with them in sun and rain."

We must work hard in any duty that God has entrusted us to do. There is a story of two children who were late for school one day. One girl said, "Let us stop and pray so that we may get to school on time." The other girl replied, "Why don't we pray as we run so that we may get to school on time?"

Darkness Hates the Light

As someone once said, it is dangerous to be too good because if you are, you are liable to be crucified. There are those who believe that there is no place for good people in the world, but only room for the mediocre.

They feel threatened in the presence of good people because they see goodness as an indictment of their own lives.

Darkness hates the light: the wicked people hated Jesus Christ, the Light of the World.

It is said that one day when Socrates was talking to his friends, one friend shouted out at Socrates, "Socrates I hate you!"

Socrates said, "I did not do you any harm."

"That is precisely it," the other man responded. "Every time I stand next to you, you threaten me because you are too good."

> *Keep shining the light of goodness so that those handicapped by darkness may catch a glimmer and be drawn to the light.*

Truth is More Valuable than Gold

As is well known, Mahatma Gandhi was a great spiritual leader of India who championed the cause of Truth in every aspect of his life. His biography is entitled, *The Experiment with the Truth.*

It is said that when Mahatma Gandhi appeared for the London Matriculation Examination, the exam paper on general knowledge contained the following question: "What is more golden than gold?"

Gandhi wrote in reply, "TRUTH."

How much more we are in need of truth in our modern world! We need more Gandhis in our lives.

Never to Yield

Gandhi was very adamant about holding onto his principles. People even called him stubborn. Gandhi's aspiration in life is summed up by his wise saying:

"To strive, to seek, to find and not to yield."

In today's society there seems to be no absolute principles, no absolute truths; everything is relative. Such a society is in great trouble.

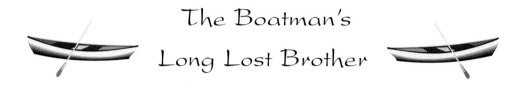

The Boatman's Long Lost Brother

There was a man who owned a boat and made a living by transporting people across the river, carrying them from one shore to the other.

One day as evening drew near, the boatman was very tired and worn out. He had worked hard for many hours, having made numerous trips from shore to shore.

As he rested in the lull of twilight, a stranger came up to him and asked the ever-familiar question, "Can you take me across the river?"

The man who owned the boat slowly shook his head in refusal, explaining, "I am very tired, but tomorrow I will take you across the river."

The stranger protested and began to rattle off several reasons why the boatman should be inclined to change his mind. "I know who you are. I know your relations. Indeed, we may be related," the stranger said. "You may be my cousin, or even my long lost brother. How can you refuse me this request?"

So the boatman reluctantly gave in and agreed to make one last trip to accommodate the stranger. During most of the crossing, the stranger was friendly and courteous. But once they neared shore, the stranger began to complain about the crossing, about the boatman's handling of the boat, and even about the boat itself.

The boatman was surprised. "Is that any way to treat your cousin, or even your long lost brother?" he asked.

"What do you mean?" the stranger replied. "I don't know you. I don't even know where you come from. Further, I have no interest in knowing anything about you."

And with that he departed the boat, without even so much as an expression of thanks or a token of gratitude.

> *Some people can be very friendly and full of compli-ments when they want something from us, but once they have satisfied their own self-interests, they become indifferent and even discourteous.*

> *Such is the nature of the world. This is why one must never put his faith in false gods. Jesus says, "If anyone serves me, let him follow me; and where I am, there my servant will be also. If anyone serves me, him my Father will honor." [John 12:26]*

The Courage of
Mahatma Gandhi

In Champaran, laborers were suffering many injustices and atrocities at the hands of the white planters. Gandhi heard of their struggle and joined them in their fight for increased rights.

One day a man came up to Gandhi and warned, "The planter of this place is the worst of the lot. He is planning to murder you. He has employed assassins."

Mahatma Gandhi feared nothing on earth but the Truth. To him, God is Truth.

So one night shortly after the man's warning, Gandhi went alone to the planter's bungalow and said, "I hear that you have employed assassins to kill me. That is why I have come alone and in secret to your house." The poor planter stood there, stunned.

*When you have God on your side and you are a
person of honesty and truth, nothing can frighten you.*

Teach My Monkey to Speak

Long ago there lived a king who kept a monkey in his palace. He was very eager to teach his monkey to speak. The king heard of a wise man who had such wonderful knowledge that he could often do things which seemed impossible. So the king invited the wise man to his palace and ordered him to teach the monkey to speak. The wise man was not sure if the king was serious, but naturally protested, "Oh! King, it is impossible to teach a monkey to speak!"

The king was indeed very serious, and as the wise man soon learned, the king would not be swayed. "Take the monkey and go away," the king insisted. "I am giving you one year. After one year is up, the monkey should be able to speak." The wise man reluctantly took the monkey and went home.

The wise man tried to the best of his ability to teach the monkey, patiently going over basic sounds and vocabulary. But the monkey refused to sit still, let alone learn, preferring to jump on books and run around the room. The monkey could not be taught so much as a single word. The wise man was so frustrated that he could not sleep or eat. His friends tried to console him, but to no avail.

After six months, the wise man returned to the king's court and asked the king for five more years to teach the monkey to speak. The king granted the extension, but still the wise man worried.

Upon his return home, the wise man's friends comforted him, saying, "Within five years anything could happen … the king could die, the monkey could die, or even you could die. Why worry about it? Take it easy, relax, and just live one day at a time."

The wise man recited this advice daily, and two years later, the wise man heard that the king had died. He and his friends threw a small party and returned the monkey to the wild.

When we worry and fret over things that may never happen in our lives, we waste the present opportunities for joy and happiness.

As Jesus says, "Do not worry about tomorrow; tomorrow will take care of itself. Sufficient for a day is its own evil." [Matthew: 6:34]

Love and
Happiness

Gandhi's Love for All

In 1922 Gandhi was sentenced to six years in prison and sent to the Yeravda Jail. The jail superintendent knew that Gandhi was loved by both Hindus and Muslims alike, so he chose an African convict, who did not speak Indian, for the service of the prisoners. So the prisoners and the attendant had to communicate with each other by gestures.

One day the African was stung by a scorpion and came running to Gandhi. Without any hesitation, Gandhi sucked the poison out of the wound and eventually the poor man began to feel better. Then Gandhi applied various other treatments and the African was relieved of his pain. It was the first time in the unfortunate man's life that he had received such love from anyone.

Truly great people never discriminate—only mean people do. When we bleed we all bleed the same blood.

The Unconditional Love of Mothers

Once upon a time there was a mother who was fast asleep on a mat, and her child was sleeping by her side. Suddenly, a snake entered the room. Some neighbors were still awake and happened to see the snake sneak inside. To alert the mother, they went near the window and shouted out her name. The mother did not respond. So then, they called her a variety of bad and foul names, but she still did not respond. Next, they found some pebbles on the ground which they threw at her through the open window. Even then she did not respond; she was in a deep sleep. The crowd was becoming increasingly impatient and fearful.

Finally, they saw some rose bushes, from which they picked some petals and threw at the child. At once the sleeping mother was aroused and screamed, "My baby! My baby!" She embraced the baby just in time to see the snake slither out the door.

A mother's love for her child is unconditional and sacrificial. When the crowd called the mother by abusive names and threw stones at her, she did not react, but when a soft rose petal fell on her child, she responded immediately. When we always put someone else before ourselves, great sacrifices become our normal way of life.

Brotherly Love

There were two brothers who loved each other very much. One brother was single and lived alone, while the other brother was married with children. Both brothers were farmers.

One year at harvest time, each brother began to think of the other. The single brother said to himself, "My brother has to provide for his wife and children, and he does not have much wealth to support them."

The married brother said to himself, "I have my wife and children to take care of me, but my poor brother has no one but himself to rely on."

So night after night, each brother would take sacks of grain from his own granary and fill his brother's granary.

Both brothers were greatly surprised that despite their nightly activities, their granaries were still always full. Curious to find out how this could be, one brother hid in his granary at night, disguised in the dark. When he saw his brother slip inside, he rushed out to embrace him. The secret that each brother had kept was evidence of the love they shared for each other. What a brotherly love it was!

True love is essential for happy families, and sharing is the joy of family life.

The Most Precious

In the heavenly court, God asked the angels what they thought was the most precious thing on earth.

One angel said, "I think the most precious thing on earth is the smile of an infant." So God ordered that a smiling infant be brought to heaven. As the angel was carrying the smiling baby boy, the baby began to change. First he grew to be a small boy, and then to an adult. The child's smile disappeared long before they got through the gate of heaven.

Another angel proposed that a beautiful rose is the most precious worldly thing, so an angel tried to carry a bouquet of roses from earth to the heavenly court. While in transit to heaven, the roses dried up and lost their beauty.

A wise angel finally said that the most beautiful and precious thing on the face of the earth must be the sacrifices made by a mother. Many angels were needed to carry all the sacrifices of mothers to the heavenly throne. When God saw the mothers' sacrifices he agreed, "Yes, indeed, the most precious thing on earth are the sacrifices made by mothers!"

And all the angels in heaven applauded.

Nothing compares to a mother's love and the sacrifices she makes for the well-being of her children. God uses mothers to pass his love on to children.

The Bridge Over Divisions

Once upon a time there lived two brothers, both of who claimed to be Catholics. But in reality, only one was a practicing Catholic.

When the brother who did not practice his faith died suddenly, his brother asked the parish priest to give him a Catholic burial. The priest refused.

So the man was buried in a non-Catholic section of the cemetery, next to a wall that divided the non-Catholics from the Catholics.

After the burial, the parish priest began to feel bad. That night, as he lay in bed, he could not sleep. With a flash of energy and urgency, he got up in the middle of the night and went to the cemetery.

He approached the grave of the dead brother, and moved the wall in such a way as to include his grave in the Catholic part of the cemetery.

The next morning the Catholic brother came to see his brother's tomb, but was dismayed when he could not find the burial spot. The priest had just entered the cemetery when he saw the Catholic brother searching frantically.

The priest came up to the young man and said soothingly, "I know what you are looking for. You are looking for your brother's tomb."

The priest then explained how he had moved the stone wall so that his brother's grave was included in the Catholic section of the cemetery.

"The law excludes by building fences," the priest said, "but love includes by moving or removing them."

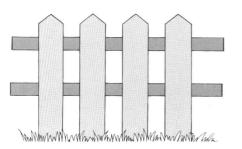

Though the law may push people away, love has the ability to draw them in.

The Sage and the Sinner

One day a holy man was walking down a street when he met a wicked man. The wicked man started to verbally abuse the holy man.

Instead of retaliating with sharp words, the holy man had only compassion for the wicked man and begged his pardon.

"I am sorry that you had to meet me," the holy man said as he walked away. The wicked man's sharp tongue sat heavy and motionless in his mouth as the holy man's words sank in.

> *Good people sometimes take upon themselves the burdens of evil people. As Jesus said, "But I say to you, love your enemies, bless those that curse you, and pray for those who spitefully use you and persecute you..." [Matthew 5:44]*

Butterflies
and Happiness

When I was a little boy in Sri Lanka, growing up in the village of Periya Kallar, I always liked to chase butterflies—I especially remember chasing butterflies by the church.

The more I chased them, the faster they flew away from me. I would get discouraged and sit on a tree stump, holding my empty bag with tight fingers.

However, when I ignored them, they would come and sit on my shoulders, and I would catch them and put them in my bag.

Happiness is something like butterflies. When we forget ourselves and get involved in helping others, then we shall find happiness. When we look for happiness with too much force, we shall not find it. So let us get involved; reach out and help others and happiness will knock at the door of your heart.

Unselfish Love

A family of elephants was traveling through the wilderness. They were all thirsty for water, for much time had passed since they last stopped at a watering hole. But, the more they looked for water, the less luck they had at finding any.

At long last they found a small puddle of water, which was only big enough for one elephant to drink. When the father elephant saw the water, he said to himself, "If I drink this water, my wife and child will go thirsty. I will just pretend to take a sip and save it for them."

His wife was the next to approach the puddle. "Oh!" she thought to herself. "If I drink the water my poor baby will die of thirst. I will just pretend to drink and save the water for my baby."

The baby elephant, unaware of his parents' sacrifice, eagerly drank up the water.

The elephant parents, in their act of selfless love, instinctively and intuitively put the welfare of their child before their own. Such consideration is fundamental for the building and maintenance of not only any strong family, but also of any stable society.

Rain and Red Soil

A young man and a young woman fell in love. Their love was so deep for each other that no other person on earth could separate them.

They went from the outskirts of their two villages to a wonderful garden. It was here that the hero expressed his ardent love for his heroine.

"We never knew each other before," he said. "Nor had we ever known or met each other's parents. Now we are related, and our love is so deep that no one on earth can separate us.

"The union of our hearts and minds is one through our love. It is like the new rainfall that comes from the sky and falls on the red soil of the earth; the rain intermingles with the red earth and it cannot be separated."

> *Love makes two separate beings inseparable. Just as the rain falls to the earth, seeps into the red soil, and cannot ever be separated from it, the union of two lovers' hearts and minds is likewise inseparable. (This story is found in Tamil Literature.)*

Happy Man without a Shirt

Once there was a king in India who asked his ministers to go around to all the towns and villages and find the happiest man in all the land. So the ministers left the palace and began their quest.

They searched high and low, far and wide, but they could not find the right man to fit the description. Even candidates who first appeared happy eventually professed some sort of desire or woe, suffering, or fear.

Finally on their way home they came upon a lone tree, under which sat a man wearing no shirt. After engaging the man in a series of dialogues and interviews, the ministers were left without any doubt that they had just spoken with the kingdom's happiest man. They brought him to the king's palace and introduced him to the king—a speechless king indeed.

> *Clothes and external adornment often serve more to mask one's inner feelings of loneliness and emptiness than they do to heighten one's feelings of content. Happiness is not something that can be worn like clothing, for it comes from the inside and cannot be put on or taken off. Happiness is a state of being, not a visually appealing aesthetic ensemble.*

Nothing Greater

According to Hindu Myth, Shiva and his wife Parvathi had two sons. The elder son was Ganesh and the younger son was Muruga.

One day Shiva and Parvathi held a competition for their sons. The prize was a very large and delicious mango. They told their two children that whoever went around the world first would receive the tasty mango. So the younger son Muruga selected a peacock as his vehicle and began his voyage around the world.

Meanwhile, the elder son Ganesh thought to himself, "Why should I go around the world? My father and my mother are my world. If I go around or circle them, then I have gone around the world!" So he ran around his mother and father, and his parents' faces lit up in smiles.

Ganesh won the prize and received the precious mango. When Muruga came home after his long trip around the world on his peacock, he was furious that his brother had won the prize. But when his parents explained to him how Ganesh had interpreted the meaning of the world, his anger subsided and he was in awe of his big brother.

> *Mothers and fathers are the center of their children's universe. When a child obeys his parents and lives by their teachings, the child is victorious in the world. But if a parent abandons his child, he tears that child's world to pieces.*

Peacocks and Celebrities

India is a land steeped in peacocks. They are of prominent cultural importance, and some cities are even named after peacocks.

A teacher was once giving a lesson on peacocks. He asked his students whether they had all seen one before. All said yes. Then he asked them whether they had ever observed a peacock's feet. Some said yes, and some said no. The teacher said that the peacock's feet are very ugly, especially compared to his beautiful feathers.

Then the teacher drew a comparison between peacocks and celebrities. He said that when a peacock is dancing, although everyone is praising his beautiful spotted feathers, inside the poor peacock is crying and ashamed that his feet are so ugly. In a similar fashion, although many people idealize celebrities for their good looks and style, we have no way of knowing what kind of pain or suffering they are harboring inside. Like the peacock, many celebrities may be putting on a great show, but secretly despising their feet, or even themselves.

Glitter, glamour, feathers, and pomp are capable of immense deceptions. All too often people assume that what is aesthetically pleasing to ours eyes is a projection of true happiness.

Wisdom
and
Humility

Humility is the Way to God

Jesus came down from heaven, an act of humility.

Jesus took on our lowly human nature, an act of humility.

Jesus was born in a stable, an act of humility.

Jesus, the Son of God, was obedient to two mortal beings. That is humility.

Jesus, who made the universe, was obedient to a carpenter. That is humility.

Jesus, who is all knowing, lived among the ignorant apostles. That is humility.

Jesus, the most loving God, walked on the dusty roads of Galilee for our sake, an act of humility.

Jesus, the almighty God, washed the feet of his apostles, an act of humility.

Jesus, the Prince of Peace, rode on a donkey, an act of humility.

Jesus died on a cross, which was intended for slaves and criminals. That is humility.

His whole life was an ongoing process of humility.

Oh proud man! Put yourself next to the Cross and see how insignificant you are. Give up your pride and learn humility.

> *None of us should glorify ourselves. Our glory is in the glory of Christ. "Humble yourselves in the sight of the Lord, and he will lift you up." [James 4:10]*

Two Brothers and a Priest

Once upon a time, two brothers lived in the same town. Although both claimed to be devout Catholics, neither one actually practiced his faith. The whole town knew them best as notorious sinners. One day the elder brother died of a heart attack, and his younger brother came to the priest with a special request.

"Father," he began, "when you give your homily at my brother's funeral mass, please say that my brother was a saint."

The priest said, "I am sorry but I simply cannot." The priest was most keenly aware of the brothers' notorious ways.

But the younger brother would not relent, and he continued to press and badger the priest, even going so far as to promise a large donation to the church if he carried out his wish. The priest found himself in a predicament.

Though he had his reservations, the man was such a pest that eventually the priest said, "Ok, I'll do my best," and shooed the man away.

When it came time for the priest to deliver his homily during the funeral mass, the younger brother sat up a bit straighter as he anticipated the ensuing accolade. The priest cleared his throat and addressed the parish with the following words:

"All of you gathered here today know the two brothers in our town. Compared to the living brother, the dead brother was a saint."

Be careful what you ask for, because sometimes you will get it, along with unexpected surprises.

The Heron's Revenge

There once was a great holy man from Tamilnadu, in the Southern part of India, who was noted for his ascetic practices and great miracles.

One day, the holy man set out early in the morning to go into a great forest, where he became engaged in deep meditation. He thought he was completely alone. His meditation, however, was suddenly interrupted when something dropped upon his head.

As the ascetic looked up, he saw a lone heron perched on a branch directly above his head, and realized that he had just been struck by bird droppings. With one sharp look the ascetic pulverized the poor bird. That was the end of the bird. Then, instead of continuing his meditation, the ascetic spent some time admiring his own spiritual power. He found himself truly impressive on occasion.

Later that day, as was his custom, the ascetic went begging in the village. He went from house to house, knocking on doors, receiving his usual provisions.

As he made his rounds, he knocked at a house where there was a long delay before any one came to the door. The ascetic grew quite impatient. What was taking so long? He knocked louder on the door, betraying his rising impatience. From inside the house, he heard a woman's voice ask, "Do you think that I am a heron?"

Her remarks astonished the ascetic, who instinctively took a step back from the door. How could this woman have known what had happened that morning in the forest; he was certain that he had been alone! The ascetic's attitude changed. He ceased knocking and waited patiently for the woman to come to the door, although inside he was burning with emotion.

When at long last she opened the door and handed him some food, the ascetic inquired about her secret knowledge. Where did she acquire the power to know things that happened in private?

"I am an ordinary housewife, faithful to my husband and to my duties," she replied. "That is my power."

The ascetic was as much surprised as he was humbled.

> *A person who humbly and faithfully carries out his or her duties may acquire knowledge and power that is beyond even a great ascetic.*

Honeybee and Taxes

There was once a great Tamil poet who gave tax instructions to the rulers of his time. He told the rulers that they had best take a lesson from the honeybee. A ruler should tax his people very gently, just like the honeybee sits on a flower without hurting the petals and gently sucks the nectar. A good ruler must tax his subjects without causing them pain.

> *We must treat those who are under our authority gently so that their spirits are nurtured and grow rather than become oppressed and stifled.*

Blessed Are the Humble

Before becoming a disciple of Rama Krishna, it is said that Vivekananda went to see this saint.

When he arrived at the saint's home, the door was shut. He knocked at the door. A voice from within inquired, "Who is there?"

The young and energetic Vivekananda answered, "I am Vivekananda." Vivekananda naturally expected the door to open, but it remained closed. He was disappointed, so he went away.

After some time, Vivekananda went again to see the great saint. As before, the door was closed. He knocked at the door. The voice from inside again questioned, "Who is there?" The young Vivekananda again replied, "I am Vivekananda." Once again the door did not budge. Vivekananda went away sad, but he began to reflect on why the master would not open the door. He then came to a startling realization: when he answered the saint's inquiry, he was emphasizing himself by responding, "I AM Vivekananda."

With this new insight he went to see the saint for a third time. Again the door was closed. The young Vivekananda knocked at the door. The voice from inside asked, "Who is there?"

The young Vivekananda replied for the first time, "Master, your servant, Vivekananda." Then to his surprise, the door was opened, the veil was removed, and young Vivekananda was able to see his master for the first time. His life was never the same after that special day.

Only when we drop our capital "I" will we be able to see God, for it is this over emphasis on ourselves that prevents us from seeing God. In the Beatitudes, Jesus says, "Blessed are the pure of heart, for they shall see God." [Matthew 5:8]

True Wisdom: Nothing Exceeds Everything

A father and his son lived in a small village. The father loved his son and was eager for him to get a solid college education. So the father sent the son to a prestigious college in another town, where he studied diligently. At the end of his first year, the son returned home for his summer vacation.

"My son, how much have you learned in your first year of college?" the father asked.

"I have learned everything, father," the son replied.

The father smiled. "Son, you have much more to learn," he said.

The father's answer puzzled the son.

After summer vacation, the son went back to the college for his second year of studies. Again, he studied diligently, and again he returned home for summer vacation. The father was very pleased to see his son.

"Son," he asked, "how much have you learned in this second year?" The son thought for a moment.

"Father, I have learned a little," he replied.

"You still have more to learn," the father said with a smile.

Two more years went by, and finally, the son completed his studies and earned his bachelor's degree.

When the son returned home, the father asked him, "Now that you have completed college, my son, tell me what you have learned?"

"Father," his son said, "I have learned that I know nothing."

Then the father embraced his son.

"Now you really have learned something. You are on your way to becoming a wise man."

The more we learn, the more we realize how little we truly know. The path to wisdom begins with recognizing our own ignorance. For how can we make room within ourselves to grow and learn when we have already put a cap on our minds?

An admission of ignorance unscrews this cap and opens up our eyes to a world of possibility. The Bible tells us that faith produces wisdom. "But the wisdom that is from above is first pure, then peaceable, gentle, willing to yield, full of mercy and good fruits, without partiality and without hypocrisy." [James 3: 17]

Lord! All I Have Written Is Straw!

St. Thomas Aquinas is considered one of the Catholic Church's greatest theologians. His Summa and other works of philosophy have been taught for the last 500 years in almost all of the world's universities. The influence of Aquinas is indeed great, but he himself was a humble man. He said that he had learned more at the foot of the Cross than anywhere else. One day when he was praying at the foot of the Cross, he had a mystical experience. Jesus spoke these words to him: "Thomas, you have written well about me. What do you want?" Thomas replied to the Lord, "Lord, all I have written is straw before you. I only want you."

> *Everything we know is insignificant before the wisdom of God. It is said that after the mystical experience St. Thomas never wrote again. We must be humble in order to experience for ourselves God's goodness and wisdom.*

 # The Fool and the King's Staff

During the Middle Ages there was a king who took great pleasure in jokes made at the expense of other people. There was a certain clown in the royal court whom the king found especially funny. One day during a big party in the royal court, the clown made the king laugh so much that the king told him, "You are the greatest fool I have ever seen in my life, here, I am giving you my staff. Keep it with you until you find a bigger fool than yourself, and then give that fool my staff." The clown took the staff from the king and went home.

Years later, the clown heard that the king was on his deathbed. He went to see the king and asked him about his health. The king said, "I am going on a long journey."

The clown asked the king whether or not he was coming back, to which the king replied, "No."

The clown then asked the king whether or not he had prepared for this long journey, and again the king's response was, "No."

The clown then bent down and spoke with deliberate force. "You mean to say that you are going to make a long journey, from which you are not coming back, and for which you are completely unprepared?" His eyes narrowed as he said without a smile, "You are the biggest fool I have ever met in my life. Here is the staff that you gave to me many years ago. Keep it." With that, the clown went away.

The wise man prepares for the future of this life and for the next.

The Elephant and the Pig

One day an elephant went out for a walk after he had just taken a bath in a lake. During his journey he came upon a bridge. As he started to walk over the bridge, a pig began to cross from the other end.

As the pig approached the elephant, the elephant stopped walking and moved to one side of the bridge, giving the pig enough room to pass.

The pig was very surprised, yet also very pleased by the elephant's behavior. The proud pig held his snout high in the air as he passed the elephant.

The pig was so filled with pride that he ran with childlike glee into the forest. He called out to all the other animals in the forest, inviting them to come and listen to his tale.

"I was walking on the bridge today," the pig said to the forest animals, "when the great elephant saw me. He was so afraid of me that he moved to one side of the bridge to let me pass."

The pig's story quickly spread throughout the forest.

The animals could hardly believe their ears, so some went to visit the elephant to see if the pig's story was indeed true.

When the great elephant heard the pig's tale, he gave a hearty laugh.

"It is true that I moved out of the pig's way when I saw him coming," the elephant said, "but I was not frightened of the pig. I had just taken a nice bath in the lake, and I did not want the filthy pig to rub against me and get me dirty."

Sometimes people get so wrapped up in pride that they are unable to see how they look to those around them.

Inflated pride leads to miscalculated judgements. All the animals knew that the elephant was bigger and stronger and wiser than the little pig, but the pig could not see how silly he looked to those around him.

"By pride comes only contention, but with the well-advised is wisdom." [Proverbs 13:10]

Gray Hair:
A Sign to Prepare for the Next Life

In the East, it is believed that once you start getting gray hair near your ears, it is time to start thinking about your next life—life after death. Rabindranath Tagore, the famous Bengali poet, used to say very humorously about this incident, "Death has placed a visiting card behind my ear."

A time comes when we must get ready for the next life. We are living in a culture that does not want to think about death. We should be ever ready to meet our Maker. As the Bible tells us, "Lord show me the shortness of my life, so that I may learn wisdom." [Psalm 90:12] To be ready is to be wise.

Responsibility
and
Respect

Crossing with the Cross

There once was a man who lived on the outskirts of a village. Every day, in order to get to his work, he had to cross a river, over which there was no bridge. But the man owned an elephant, and each day he would ride his elephant while another man held onto the elephant's tail. In this fashion, the two men and the elephant safely crossed the river.

Day after day, a third man, who lived near the river, watched this scene take place. This man owned a dog. Though his dog was not nearly as large or strong as the elephant, the man kept thinking to himself, "Why can't I hold on to my dog's tail as he swims across the river? If the man with the elephant can do it, why can't I?"

So one day the man decided to cross the river, holding onto the dog's tail as it swam to the other side. His experiment was a disaster; both he and his dog drowned in their attempt to mimic the man with the elephant.

Life is like a river that we must cross. In order to get from one bank to the other, we must have the right equipment. Though many people are deceived into believing that worldly goods are sufficient for our journey, if we want to safely cross the divide, we must hold on to one thing: the precious Cross of Christ. The power in the Cross is what enables us to complete our journey, taking us through the waters of life to the divine destination of Heaven.

You Could Have Hissed

Once there was a poisonous snake who terrorized a certain village and killed many people. One day a holy man of God passed through the village. The people came to the holy man and complained about the poisonous snake, begging him to take action against the snake. The holy man called the snake aside and warned him not to bite the people.

The snake promised not to bite any more living creatures and to live instead by eating herbs.

The holy man blessed the snake and went away, yet promised to return and see the snake in the future.

The snake left the village and went to live in a cave. One day as the snake lay in the sun outside the cave, some boys from the village spotted him from a distance. They began to throw stones at the snake. Instead of attacking the boys, as in the days before, the snake slowly slithered into the cave without harming anyone.

As the weeks, months, and years passed, the boys from the village became more and more bold. They began to harass the serpent on a daily basis, twisting his tail and throwing stones at him. But the serpent did not retaliate. Instead, he tried to hide by slithering from bush to bush, or hiding in the shadows of trees.

After a few years, the holy man passed through the village again. He stopped and inquired about the snake. The people told the holy man that the snake was in bad shape. He was no more than skin and bones, and because he spent all his time trying to hide from the boys, he hardly had time to look for food.

So the holy man approached the snake. He asked the snake what had happened to him. The snake replied that he had been very obedient to the holy man's words and had never harmed or bit anyone since his initial warning. Nevertheless, he was sickly and close to death.

The holy man shook his head. "I told you not to bite, but I did not tell you not to hiss. If you had hissed, you would have prevented this situation from happening to you."

So the holy man blessed the snake and continued on his journey.

By telling others when their actions displease us, we may avoid future discomfort.

The Empire and the Nail

Imagine a battle scene. Two emperors from two different countries are fighting. They are on their horse-driven chariots. One emperor cannot fight well because one of the nails from one of his horse's shoes was lost. Because the nail was lost, the shoe was lost. Because the shoe was lost, the horse was lost. Because the horse was lost, the chariot was lost. Because the chariot was lost, the emperor was lost. Because the emperor was lost, the whole kingdom was lost.

If we are not careful about the little things, the biggest things can be lost.

At My Side

The book of Genesis tells us that God created the first woman not from the head or feet of man, but from his side. There is deep meaning in this act.

Suppose God had created the first woman from the man's head, then she could be superior to the man, and be full of pride and boasting. (Thank God it did not happen this way.)

And yet, if God had created the woman from the man's feet, then he could call her inferior and walk all over her. (Thank God this did not happen, either.)

Rather, in his infinite wisdom the Almighty God created woman from the side of man. The side is a symbolically rich part of our body: We always wish to keep our closest friends, helpers, and partners "at our side."

Woman is friend, companion, and helpmate to man. She is a friend with whom to eat bread.

Woman is a wonder of God's handiwork. Remembering the story of creation helps us to have the right perspective on life.

[This interpretation is attributed to St. Augustine.]

Your Freedom Ends
Where My Nose Begins

A certain man was walking down the street, swinging his walking stick. While he was swinging the stick, it struck the nose of a man who was walking a few paces behind him. Holding his nose, he shouted out to the man with the walking stick, "Sir, please pay attention to how you swing your walking stick because it just struck me on my nose!"

The man with the walking stick was not pleased at having been publicly reprimanded and replied with an air of disgust, "Who are you to question me? It is my freedom to swing my walking stick wherever I want."

"Yes! What you say is true." The other man replied. "But, your freedom ends where my nose begins!"

> *Freedom is not being able to do whatever we want to do, whenever we want to do it. Rather, true freedom is doing what we ought to do, and simultaneously respecting the freedom of others.*

Fool's Gold

Long ago in India, a king lived in a magnificent palace near Madras City. Next door to the palace, there lived a saintly man who loved to chant songs in praise of God. He chanted at any hour day or night.

The king was disturbed by these chants, and on many nights, he could not sleep. He complained to his ministers, and one wise minister told the king not to worry. "I shall take care of it," he calmly reassured the king.

The minister approached the saintly man and gave him a bag of gold. The holy man could not believe his good fortune!

Once alone, he dug a hole in the ground, buried the bag of gold, and sat on it. At night, he would steal into the dark with his shovel and creep to his special spot, where he would unearth the bag of gold and carry it inside to put under his bed.

This behavior went on for several months. The king, out of curiosity, finally asked the minister, "What did you do to stop the holy man from singing?"

The minister smiled and said, "I have given the holy man a bag of gold, and this distraction is keeping his tongue silent."

Enraptured by the gleam of his gold, the holy man was turning his back on God.

No one is immune to temptation; even a saint can become distracted if he does not keep his eyes and mind firmly focussed on God.

The Rich Man and His Walking Stick

There was once a rich man in a village who was very proud of his wealth and power. And he did not care very much for his village folks.

Whenever anyone died in the village, people would send word to him asking him to come to the funeral. Instead of attending these events himself, the rich man would simply send his walking stick to represent him. He did this on all occasions, so as not to waste his own precious time, unaware of the insult felt by his fellow villagers.

One day the rich man died, and the news of his death was announced to all the villagers. The villagers joined together and sent their own walking sticks to his funeral. Not a single person attended the funeral to pay their respects. Instead, his coffin was surrounded by piles of walking sticks.

If you care for people when you are living, they will care for you in return; you receive what you give. Pay attention to how you treat people. "as a man sows so shall he reap." [Galatians 6:7]

The Monkey and the Crocodile

Once upon a time, a big crocodile lived in the river of Sri Lanka. Growing alongside the river were many trees bearing very tasty purple berries. A large community of monkeys made their home in the branches of these berry-laden trees.

One of these monkeys became friendly with the big crocodile. The monkey would feed the crocodile berries, and in exchange the crocodile would carry the monkey on his back across the river wherever he wanted to go. The two unlikely creatures became chummy. The crocodile would always take some of the berries home to his crocodile wife, who enjoyed the berries as much as her big husband, although she never ate quite as many.

One morning Mrs. Crocodile told her husband, "Honey! These berries are so delicious, just think how much sweeter the liver of the monkey must be—he eats so many berries! I would like to taste that monkey's liver. Please bring him home to me."

Mr. Crocodile could not believe his ears. He protested vehemently, "No, I could never do that to my friend!" His wife narrowed her eyes and said, "Then you don't love me as before. If you really loved me, you would bring the monkey home to me. Prove your love to me!" Crushed under the pressure, he reluctantly promised to bring the monkey home that evening.

That afternoon when the two bumped into each other along the bank of the river, Mr. Crocodile very cunningly told the monkey, "My wife wants to give you a party tonight! As my friend, you are most welcome to come to our home." The monkey was very pleased with the invitation and immediately accepted. So the crocodile chauffeured the monkey on his back down the river. During the ride the monkey asked the crocodile, "So what is the menu for dinner tonight?"

The crocodile said, "Liver!"

"Liver?" the monkey asked, "Whose liver?"

"Your liver," the crocodile said. "My wife thinks that since you are always eating those tasty berries, your liver must be very, very delicious. So I am taking you to her."

The monkey drew in a quick breath. He realized that he was trapped on the back of a crocodile in the middle of a deep river, with no escape route. But he did not panic, instead he used his wit and said, "I am sorry, but my liver is not here; it is on the top of the purple berry tree where I live. If you take me back to the tree, then I shall get it for your wife."

The foolish crocodile believed the monkey's tale. The crocodile turned around and swam back to the tree. As soon as they skidded to a stop on the bank of the river, the monkey jumped off his betrayer's back and yelled, "How ungrateful you are! I fed berries to you and your family, and now you want to eat my liver? Be gone you false friend!"

The monkey climbed to the very top of the tree, rallied his friends and family around him, who joined him in chanting, "Be gone you false friend!"

We must be careful in choosing our friends. Once we are trapped with bad friends it is always difficult to escape.

Tales from the Heart

Hunger for Harmony

Long ago in ancient Italy, the villagers and townspeople became very discontent. They squabbled among themselves about who was more important. They also resented the authority of the central government and became so discontented and resentful that they refused to pay taxes.

A wise man saw that there was great disorder among the people. He wanted to restore harmony and order, so he gathered together all the people and told them a story:

"Once upon a time, all the parts of the body decided to hold a meeting. The two feet, the two hands, the mouth, tongue, teeth, two eyes, and two ears came together for a discussion.

"Soon they all began to complain, and the target of their complaints was the stomach. First to speak were the feet, 'We have to work very hard to get food, and we have to walk long distances to get the food and bring it back.'

" 'We work hard too,' said the hands. 'We have to hold the large bundles while the feet bring the entire body back to our home.'

"All the other parts of the body sympathized with the feet and the hands. And they, too, explained how hard they worked for food. The stomach was accused of extreme laziness. 'The stomach does not work like us,' the others said. 'It just stays in one place and benefits from all our hard work.'

"Finally, all the parts of the body agreed to teach the stomach a lesson. They decided they would no longer provide food for the lazy stomach.

" 'We will not walk to the market to buy food,' the feet said.

" 'We will not carry the food,' the hands said.

" 'I won't open to let the food in,' the mouth said.

" 'I will not bite into the food and grind it,' the teeth said.

"And so they all agreed to go on a hunger strike to punish the stomach and to teach it a lesson.

"After a few days, the parts of the body became very weak. The feet began to stagger and the hands shook. The eyes dimmed and the teeth began to ache.

"So the parts of the body held another meeting. 'We have in fact learned a great lesson,' the feet said. 'We give the stomach food, and the stomach gives us energy and health. We did not understand that the stomach contributes as much as we do.'

"All the other parts of the body agreed. They ended their hunger strike, and health and harmony were restored to the body."

After the wise man told this story, the people of the villages and towns soon realized that they, too, had made a mistake—they were punishing themselves with useless squabbling, and they were punishing a system that was really in place to keep their lives running smoothly. And so once they stopped their internal fighting and adopted a new attitude toward the central government, order and harmony were restored in the villages and towns.

In order to have a good society, we each have an important role to play. We must have many different people who perform many different jobs. It is not important as to which job is of the most significance, but rather, how all the various jobs work to achieve a greater goal. The larger unifying vision is only as strong as each of its various components. That is why our Creator has produced such diverse human beings.

"The commandments ... are summed up in this saying, 'You shall love your neighbor as yourself.'" [Romans 13:9]

The Monk and the Monkey

There was a monk who lived in a forest, and every day, he spent time in prayer and meditation. As he meditated, he always kept a water jar and a stick next to him.

In the same forest, there lived a monkey who was fascinated by the monk.

One day the monkey crept up to the monk and quietly stared at him. The monk did not pay any attention to the monkey.

The next day, the monkey crept still closer to the monk. This time, he made faces at the monk. But still the monk did not pay any attention to the monkey.

On the third day, the monkey jumped onto the lap of the monk, and still the monk did not acknowledge the monkey.

On the fourth day, the monkey became even more bold and jumped onto the shoulder of the monk. But the monk still ignored the monkey.

On the fifth day, the monkey took the water jar, jumped on the monk's head, and poured the water all over him. The monk took the stick and hit the monkey, and the monkey quickly ran away.

We should know when to take action. If the monk had reprimanded the monkey on the first day, he would never have gotten wet. It is always wise to resist evil from the very beginning.

Frog or Bee Mentality

There once was a pond in a small village that had many water lilies. Amongst the water lilies there lived some frogs, who did not know the value of the water lilies, nor did they appreciate their sweet scented perfume. The water lilies were such a common part of the frog's environment that they had practically stopped noticing them altogether.

The honeybees, who lived far away in the lofty hills of Pothikai, or the hills of Tamilnadu in South India, heard about the pond's beautiful water lilies and flew thousands of miles just to enjoy their nectar. Although the honeybees had weary wings after such a journey, when they sat on the water lilies and sipped the nectar, they were all at peace. The frogs went about their business, noticing nothing but perhaps an increased buzzing in the air.

> *When we live near a special person or place, we may take them for granted and forget how wonderful they are. Others who hear of their greatness may travel from distant places at great personal cost, just to see the special person or place up close. Do you have a frog or a honeybee mentality?*
>
> *"No prophet is without honor except in his own country, among his own people." [John 4:44]*

Spirit of Charity, Compassion and Kindness

The King and the Hawk

Once upon a time in India, there lived a king named Sibi Chackaravathi who was just and kind to his subjects.

One afternoon when he was in his portico, a shivering dove came flying in through the window and rested on his shoulder. Pursued by a hungry hawk, the dove came seeking safety and protection.

The dove had hardly alighted on the king's shoulder and explained her plight before her pursuer arrived, squawking and causing an uproar. "King please give me my food! I am hungry. By giving sanctuary to the dove, you are depriving me of my food. The people say you are a just king—and yet you deny me my food?"

The king and the hawk began a very heated argument on ethics and morality. The hawk said, "It is my right to get food. I hunted my food very diligently, but now you are preventing me from eating."

"Go and eat some worms," the king said.

The hawk scowled and said, "I am the king of birds! We don't settle for such cheap food. Because we are so very sporty, we fight to get our delicious food."

The king then offered to give him a rat or a mouse.

Again the hawk insisted, "I am the king of birds! I eat only royal food." Then the king got a strange look in his eye; he offered the hawk his own flesh.

To this the hawk consented. The king's servants brought out a scale. On one side they put the dove, and on the other side they put a pound of flesh from the king's hand. They weighed them; they were equal. The pound of king's flesh was then awarded to the hawk, the king of the birds. The hawk was satisfied with the deal, and flew away with his new meal in his mouth. The noble king saved the life of the dove.

Compassion and selfless sacrifice towards God's creatures is the truly noble and royal mode of living.

Gandhi and His Shoes

One day Mahatma Gandhi was waiting for a train in New Delhi. When he boarded the train and it began to pull away, he looked down at his feet and realized that he had left one of his shoes back on the platform. He immediately took off the remaining shoe and threw it outside, where it landed next to the other shoe.

When another passenger questioned him, "Why did you do that?" Gandhi's response was that if a poor person found the shoes, then he would have a complete pair to wear.

Magnanimous and noble people always think about others, especially those less fortunate.

The Truck Driver and the Priest

A truck driver and a priest died on the same day, and both went to heaven. The truck driver got a higher place in heaven than the priest. When the priest discovered this, he became very unhappy.

One day, as Jesus went around heaven meeting people, he came upon the priest and asked him how he was enjoying eternity. Instead of responding with joy, the priest could not hide his annoyance with Jesus.

"What's the trouble?" Jesus asked.

The priest tried to hold his tongue, but could not. He complained to Jesus, "I consecrated my whole life to serving you. But now I come to heaven and I find that a truck driver has been given a higher place in heaven than me."

Then Jesus asked the priest, "What am I to do? Every time you preached, people fell asleep; but whenever they saw the truck driver driving, the people prayed."

Boring sermons do not draw people closer to God.

The Life Giving Tree

Once upon a time, there was a little boy named Jimmy who had a big oak tree in his backyard. Jimmy would climb up into the tree's branches and play for hours. He loved the tree very much, and the oak tree also loved him. They became great friends. After days when Jimmy did not come to play on its branches, the tree would ask him, "Where were you yesterday? I was waiting for you."

One day Jimmy told the oak tree that it was time for him to start school. He gave the oak tree a big hug and kiss.

On the first day of school, Jimmy's teacher told the class that each student must bring in money the next day to pay for textbooks. Jimmy was very worried about this because he and his family had very little money. In the evening he came home sad and went directly to the backyard to sit under his friend the oak tree.

"Jimmy why are you sad?" the oak tree asked. "What is troubling you?"

"I have no money to buy my textbooks," Jimmy explained, "and the teacher said that if you can't afford the textbooks, then you shouldn't bother coming to school."

"Look up," the oak tree told him. "See my little branches? Cut them and sell them so you can buy the textbooks."

Jimmy did just as the oak tree instructed him to do. Over the years, Jimmy did well in school and grew to be both wise and strong. He finished school and went on to high school. Every evening he never failed to come and talk and play with the tree. One day he fell in love with a beautiful girl, much to his and the tree's delight. One evening, though, he came with a sad face to the tree and told him that he had had a quarrel with his girlfriend. The tree consoled him, and after some time Jimmy married his high school sweetheart. The tree blessed the new couple.

Years later, Jimmy lost his job. He was sad and frustrated, and came to sit under the oak tree. The tree asked him, "Why are you sad, Jimmy?"

"I've lost my job, and I don't know what to do."

"I am here for you," the tree told him. "Cut my big branches and limbs. Then, you can make a big boat to earn your living."

So Jimmy cut down the tree's big limbs and left only the stump of the tree. He made a big boat and left the place for good with his wife.

After many years had passed, Jimmy lost his wife and everything else he had in life. He came to the old oak tree a tired old man. There was nothing left of the tree except the stump. Still the oak was delighted to see his old friend. "I am still here for you," the tree said. "I offer you my stump—please come and rest awhile."

The oak tree gave everything of itself to his friend—
even its stump. We should all be like this life-giving tree.

The Chieftain's Love for a Creeper

There once lived a chieftain by the name of Paari, from the southern part of India. Paari was a selfless man, and he was most noted for his selfless love. One day he was riding in his chariot when he saw a kind of creeper—a plant called a Mullai, which grows in Tamilnadu.

The creeper was reaching its branches upwards toward the light. As Paari was very tenderhearted, he could feel the creeper searching for a sunlit place to rest. So Paari stopped his chariot at such a place which enabled the creeper to climb on it. Paari left the chariot for the creeper and went home by foot.

The chieftain saw the creeper as not just an inconsequential thing, but as a part of the universe in which he lived. His love for this world compelled him to protect the creeper vine.

Although we today may scoff at his actions for being absurd, the people of his time saw life in nature and embraced the whole of creation with utter tenderness.

The Worshipping Hands

Albrecht Durer, the famous sculptor and painter, grew up longing to study sculpture at the Vienna School, as did his brother. But since their family was very poor, they could not afford to send either son to the school. So the two brothers made an agreement: one would go to work and support the other brother, who would go to study in Vienna. When that brother returned from school, the two would swap places, and the other brother would have his turn to study sculpture. By chance, Albrecht Durer was chosen first to go to Vienna to study painting and sculpture, while his brother worked hard in the mines to support him.

After his studies were complete, Albrecht Durer came home. His family threw him a big reception to honor his achievement. During the party he saw his brother, who had sacrificed so much for him and who had worked such long hours in the mines, hiding his hands. When Albrecht Durer saw his brother's hands, he saw a gnarled and crooked distortion of what his brother's hands once were. He was deeply touched by his brother's sacrifice. He went into the studio and sculpted an image of the worshipping hands as a sign of his love and gratitude to his brother.

True brotherly love is sacrificial and self-effacing.

The Beggar's Divine Comedy

One day I was begging from house to house when suddenly I saw a golden chariot coming towards me. "Who is this king?" I wondered. My hopes soared high as I thought to myself, "Today could be the last day of my begging. My pain and poverty may finally come to an end. Without asking, I may get some gold from this king! The road will be scattered with precious stones, and all because this king is advancing in a golden chariot."

As I was imagining all of these things in my heart, the golden chariot, which was quickly approaching, lurched to a stop right next to me. The king inside glanced down and smiled at me. "Today may be the luckiest day of my life," I thought, prepared to accept all sorts of gifts.

Suddenly from within the chariot, the king reached out his bejeweled right hand towards me and asked, "What offering do you have for me?" I drew a short breath—I was so very confused. Is it not divine comedy to ask for alms from a beggar who is in turn asking for alms?

Grudgingly, I took one of the grains from my bag and thrust it into the outstretched palm of the king. The king and his gleaming chariot moved off at once, turned around a bend, and disappeared from my sight. I did not move a step. I was devastated.

In the evening when I reached my hut, I lit my little lamp and opened the bag of grain. As I emptied it, I saw a miracle: dispersed amidst the grains, glittered a little gold coin. I lamented and wept that I did not have the heart to give you all that I had in my bag.

God comes to us in so many different ways that we cannot even begin to imagine them all. He is more generous to us than we are to him. Ask him for a giving heart.

The Nature of a True Friend

One day a great sage in Tamilnadu, South India, had a discussion on friendship. The sage drew an analogy between friendship and modesty. When one's clothes loosen and fall, at once the hand reaches out to hold the dress in order to protect the body's honor. So, too, when a sorrow afflicts a friend, a true friend will go at once to try and rescue his friend from harm.

A true friend will be there for you to protect you from disgrace and shame, just like the hand that rushes out immediately to protect the body from public scrutiny.

 # Pigs Don't Pray

One day a man traveled from his village into town to do some shopping. He was hungry after having finished his errands, so he went to a restaurant and ordered a hot meal. Before he began to eat, he bent his head in prayer and said grace. Some other men in the restaurant saw the stranger praying, and began to make fun of him. As they laughed and snickered, they asked him, "Does everyone do this where you come from?" Very calmly the man replied, "The pigs don't."

Everyone should be thankful to God for what he gives us and show this appreciation by saying grace before meals. If we don't, how are we any different from pigs?

Know Your Origins

According to Hindu legend, a group of hunters once invaded a palace, stole all of its treasures, and then set it on fire. Many of those who resided in the palace were killed, though the king and the queen did manage to escape. Their infant prince, however, was captured by the hunters and taken to live among them. The young prince grew up with the other boys, learning the art of hunting and war. He knew nothing of his royal lineage. He became a great hunter among the hunters.

As years passed, the people of the country began again to look in earnest for the prince. His father was getting old, and as the rightful successor to the throne, the kingdom was anxious to restore him to his place. A thorough search was conducted throughout the country.

The king and the wise men finally discovered the hunters' head-quarters, where they met the young prince in the form of a hunter. He looked just as his father had looked twenty years prior, at the time of the raid.

The king dispelled his son's ignorance and convinced him that he belonged not to a hunting clan, but to the royal clan. His long-await-ed return was greeted with much celebration and festivity, and he was soon crowned king of the country.

> *We all belong to royal lineage. God is our king. We are all created in the image and likeness of our heavenly Father. Paradise belongs to us. Although sin entered the world, and Satan deceived us, Jesus is our divine teacher who dispels our ignorance and sin through his redemption. He informs us of our divine origin. Know your origin! You are a prince! You are a princess!*

The Monk and
the Scorpion

Near the holy river Ganges a monk was absorbed in deep meditation. When he opened his eyes he saw a scorpion struggling to get out of the river and onto the shore. Although he knew full well that the scorpion's nature is to sting, he felt sorry for it just the same and went to help it. He took it in his hands very gently and placed it on the bank of the river. Then he sat back down to continue his meditation. After a while, he opened his eyes, and again he saw the scorpion struggling, this time to get back into the river. He got up, took the scorpion in his hands and placed it in the water. Every time he took the scorpion into his hands it stung him. This scenario took place many times at this holy river.

Another man who had been observing the monk's actions finally went up to him and scolded, "You are very foolish. Don't you know that the nature of scorpions is to sting? Why are you helping it?"

The monk smiled and said, "Yes, you are right, the nature of the scorpion is to hurt, but my nature is to help. I will not allow the scorpion to supersede me. I shall keep on helping. That is my nature."

We have to overcome evil by good. There will be lots of people we meet in our lives who will be like scorpions, consistently hurting us, but we have to go on helping them. God expects this from us.

The Puppy and the Barnyard Animals

There once was a man with a large barnyard, in which he kept all sorts of horses, donkeys, cattle, and sheep. One day, he brought a puppy home to his barnyard. The puppy was very excited and began to run about the barnyard, unwittingly making the other animals uncomfortable by his displays of energetic zest.

One day when the master went to work, all the other animals began to make fun of the new puppy. The horse shot him a low look and said, "My master goes racing on me."

The donkey followed suit and sneered, "My master carries lots of heavy things on me."

The cow heaved in one breath, "I give plenty of milk for the whole family."

And the big tough dog flexed his muscles and said, "The master depends on me to guard the house."

One by one all of the other animals bragged about how valuable they were to the master. Together they implored, "What can you do? Oh! Little puppy, what can you do for the master?"

The puppy felt sad and was at a loss for words, so he went to a corner and lay down and slept.

That evening, the master was so tired when he came home from work that he immediately sat down in his easy chair. When the puppy saw his mas-

ter, he rose from the corner and ran over to play. The master and the puppy rolled around on the ground and played.

The puppy kissed the master and the master hugged the puppy. He carried the puppy in his arms around the barnyard, while all the other animals stared on in amazement. They overheard the master murmur to the puppy, "I shall not trade you for all the animals in the world, because you bring me more joy than all the other animals combined."

The other animals felt shame for their conduct, and secretly wished it was they who brought the master such joy.

> *Our society routinely and explicitly esteems a person's worth solely by means of his achievements and possessions, and not for who or what he is. Such traits as goodness, kindness, and the ability to bring joy cannot be tabulated. Any appraisal of character which overlooks these traits, however, is no real appraisal in the eyes of God.*

A Question of Possession

Once upon a time a mother had a very beautiful daughter. She showered all her love onto her child. One day without telling her mother, the daughter eloped with her boyfriend. The mother was incredibly distraught when her daughter did not come home, and she began to look for her everywhere. Along the way, the mother confronted a wise man. The wise man asked the mother why she was so upset. After the mother told the wise man the whole story about her daughter leaving home, the wise man gave her the following advice.

"The pearl, even though it is born in the deep ocean, does not belong to the ocean. It belongs to the one who wears it around her neck strung from a chain.

"Likewise the sandalwood, although it is born in the forest, does not belong to the forest. It belongs to the person who makes it into a powder and applies it onto her body.

"The music from a flute, even though it is created in the flute, does not belong to the flute. Rather, it belongs to the one who listens to the music. Even though your daughter was born and raised in your home, like the pearl, the sandalwood, and the flute, she now belongs to another home. Now you may go in peace," the wise man said.

A mother cannot hold onto her daughter forever. A time comes when the daughter needs to make her own home. (This story is told in Tamil literature).

The Chieftain and the Honeybees

A certain chieftain from the first century A.D., in Tamilnadu, India, was well known for his tenderness and generosity.

According to legend, his kindness was even extended to birds and animals. It is said that one day, as the chieftain was going home in a chariot, his charioteer was riding fast and ringing a bell very loudly. When they passed through a grove, the chieftain noticed two bees mating. Since he did not want to disturb them, he told the charioteer to stop ringing the bell immediately, and to drive as slowly as he could. He knew that if the bees were disturbed they would fly away. Such was his tenderness for the honeybees.

We all need to be sensitive to the whole of creation around us. We are living in a society where too many people are not sensitive to one another. We have to respect not only ourselves, but also the lives of others.

God's Presence

The Boy and His Kite

A small boy was once flying a kite in the sky. He held onto the string tightly and watched the kite soar in the sky. Suddenly a few stray clouds came by and covered the kite.

A man passed by and asked the boy, "Boy! What are you doing?"

"I am flying my kite," the boy said. The man looked up at the sky, but the cloud hid the kite. "I don't see anything up there," the man said.

"Even though I don't see anything now, I know my kite is there because every now and then I feel a pull on the string," the boy replied as he turned away from the man and back to his kite.

At times we may not feel the presence of God in our lives, but he is there. We feel the pull of him, so long as we are open to his mystery.

First Snow

There was a priest who grew up in Sri Lanka and later lived in India. He never saw snow firsthand. He had only seen it in movies and in magazines.

When he came to the United States in 1984, he was assigned to a parish in the Bronx and lived at St. Mary's Rectory, in the East Bronx.

In November, the first snow of the year began to fall. The priest was in his room on the third floor. When he looked through the window and saw sheets of snow falling to the ground, he closed the curtains and called anxiously to the rectory cook over the intercom.

"Please come immediately to my room!" he shouted. "I am in big trouble!"

The seventy-year-old cook climbed up to the third floor, probably envisioning a rat or some other frightening rodent under the bed. She came to the door shouting, "Father, what's the matter?"

The priest opened the curtains and showed her the snow scene.

"What's that?" he asked.

"It is snow, Father."

Without explaining himself any further, he ran like a child down the stairs and out the door and began to play in the snow. The cook was confused. She went and told the pastor that there was a crazy priest living in the rectory. It was only after she told the pastor the whole story that the pastor realized the priest had just come from Sri Lanka and snow was a foreign substance to him.

In this world as we grow into adults we lose that sense of wonder toward God's creation. We have to kindle within us this precious wonder of life.

A Gentle Slap

When I was in Singapore with my friend Father Aloysius Doraisarny at Our Lady of Lourdes Church, there was a certain gentleman who frequently annoyed me. "Father Antony," he would say, "there is no God. Don't waste your time!"

I told him that there is a God. But that the idea of God cannot be defined, just like the love between two lovers cannot be defined. Devotees of God experience a similar sensation.

This man was not satisfied by my answer. He kept doubting and denying the existence of God. "What proof can you supply?" he demanded.

So one day, he irritated me so much that I gave him a gentle slap on the cheek.

"Father," he said, "that hurt!"

I told him to prove it to me.

"I cannot prove it," he said. "I just experience the pain."

I told him that now he knew how devotees of God feel. The intensity of pain and joy cannot be proven, only experienced. God is someone we experience.

We experience God; we don't prove him. One's relationship with God cannot be defined.

The Treasure Is in You

There once lived a Rabbi Eisik, who was the son of Rabbi Jekel of Krakow. Rabbi Eisik had a dream. He dreamt the same dream three times. In the dream he saw a treasure that was buried under the bridge that led to the king's castle in Prague.

Rabbi Eisik was determined to go and dig up the treasure, so he traveled to Prague. But when he came to the bridge, he found that it was heavily guarded. He returned daily, hoping for an opportunity to dig for the treasure. Finally, the captain of the guards asked him why he kept loitering by the bridge. So Rabbi Eisik told him of his dream.

The captain laughed at the Rabbi for believing in dreams, and in order to show that it was ridiculous to pay attention to dreams, he recounted one of his own.

The captain said that he himself had dreamt of a treasure hidden in Krakow, in the house of a Jewish man named Eisik, son of Jekel. In his dream the treasure was buried in a dirty corner behind the stove. The Rabbi thanked the captain and quickly returned home, where he found the treasure exactly where the captain had dreamt it to be.

Our true treasure is not far from us; it is within us. As Jesus said, "...for indeed, the kingdom of God is within you." [Luke 17:21] It lies deep in our heart of hearts, we only need to find a way to tap into it. You don't have to go too far—the treasure is within you!

The Pumpkin and the Acorn

There once was a man who saw a big pumpkin on a tiny vine and a small acorn on a big tree. He said to himself, "If I were God I would reverse the order. I would put the big pumpkin on the big tree and the small acorn on the tiny vine. That would be the right way to create. God's way does not make any sense."

That summer afternoon, he set off by foot on a long journey to another village. He became so tired after walking for a while that he decided to take a nap under an oak tree. During his sleep something fell on his head and disturbed his rest. He woke up to see an acorn at his side. As he rolled the light acorn between his fingers, he realized the wisdom of Almighty God, and said to himself, "Thank God it was not a pumpkin, my head would have been smashed to pieces—no, make that pumpkin seeds!"

God knows what he is doing. His ways are not our ways, rather, they are inscrutable, true, and everlasting. In Scripture it says, "For as the heavens are higher than the earth, so are my ways higher than your ways." [Isaiah 55:9]

St. Francis and the Crabs

When I was studying at Madras University, I heard that the people of Tuticorin, a coastal area near Tamilnadu, did not eat a certain kind of crab.

As a university student, I would not allow myself to believe such a merely provincial superstition. But one day, I traveled to the beaches of Tuticorin and talked to some of the local fishermen. They picked up a few crabs and brought them over to me, showing me that some of the crabs had cross marks on their hard shells. I learned that the people of that area do not eat those crabs as a mark of respect to St. Francis Xavier.

According to legend, St. Francis Xavier loved his crucifix very much, which is why we always see him depicted with the crucifix. One day when he was travelling by ship, he accidentally dropped his crucifix in the sea, and was remarkably upset. But when he got off the boat and reached the shore, a lone crab was crawling on the sand with the crucifix held between his two tentacles. St. Francis Xavier was overjoyed and blessed the crab by the sign of the cross on his back.

Simple people can often see the hand of God in many things, whereas those who consider themselves sophisticated may not see him at all. As Robert Browning would say, "The earth is crammed with heaven, he who has eyes to see will take off his shoes."

God in All Things

A spiritual master taught his disciples that God is in all things—in everything. A certain disciple listened to this teaching very carefully and decided to put it into practice.

One day the disciple was walking on a trail in a forest. Suddenly he heard a voice crying out, "Move to the side! Move to the side! An uncontrollable elephant is coming down the road!"

This disciple did not move. He said to himself, "My master told me that God is in everything. He said I should see God in all things. So I will see God in this elephant, and I will not move from the road."

The mahout, which is the name given to an elephant driver, again gave a warning, "Move to the side! Move to the side!"

But the disciple refused to move.

The elephant rushed upon the disciple, and with his trunk, the elephant picked up the disciple and threw him to the ground, knocking him unconscious.

The disciple was taken to the hospital. When he awoke, he began to curse the master. The other disciples reported this matter to the master, who shortly after came to see the injured disciple.

The disciple was very angry and at first refused to speak to the master. The master waited patiently, and finally the disciple began to complain. "You said that God is in everything. So I saw God in the elephant, and I did not move. See what has happened to me!"

"Ah," the master said, "you saw God in the elephant, and that is good. But God also came to you in the voice of the mahout! Why didn't you listen to him and move to the side?"

God speaks to us through wise and holy people. We must be able to discern his voice; listening is in and of itself a very important action.

Hippy or Happy

One day a happy saint met an unhappy hippy. The frowning hippy asked the saint, "Why is it that you smile all the time and are so happy with your life?"

"Why, you ask?" responded the saint. "It is because we saints focus on the second letter of the word 'happy'—the letter 'A' which stands for Alpha, which in turn stands for God. That is why we are happy."

"And what about us hippies? Why do I feel light years away from happiness?"

The saint drew a breath and explained, "Perhaps it is because hippies focus on the second letter of the word 'hippy'—the letter 'I.' That is, people who concentrate more on themselves than on God will not be truly happy."

When we focus on God and on our brothers and sisters, rather than ourselves, happiness will follow.

The Hand Print of God

Once upon a time a young maiden fell in love with a young man from a neighboring village. Dividing the two lovers was a huge mountain, through which flowed a magnificent waterfall. The waterfall brought flowers, leaves, and stones from the young man's village to his beloved's village further down stream. The young maiden would collect these flowers, leaves, and stones like precious treasures and keep them in her home. The mountain and all of nature's objects reminded her of her lover. Because of her great love for him, all of the things from his village were sacred to her and she cherished them. Her eyes filled with tears when she watched the mountain waterfall because it also reminded her of her lover.

Just like the objects of her lover's village reminded the maiden of her lover, so does the devotee of the Lord see the Divine Lover in all objects of creation. Creation is the hand print of God. The devotee of the Lord sheds tears in love and wonder at God's manifold gifts.

Unaware of God's Omniscience

There was once an Indian boy who was taken into the jungle on his thirteenth birthday. According to the customs of his tribe, a boy's courage must be tested before he is granted full membership in the tribe.

To test his courage, the boy was left alone in the jungle for the whole night. He never thought that the night could be so long! He was frightened by strange noises, watched dark shapes blow in the night air, and could hardly bring himself to close his eyes. He thought morning would never come, but he refused to return to his village.

Morning did eventually come, and as his eyes became accustomed to the dawn's early light, he looked around and was amazed to find that standing behind a tree to his immediate right was his own father. His father first congratulated him on his display of courage, then explained that he had been on duty all night, with a gun, standing guard.

The boy's first reaction was to think to himself, "Well, if I had known that he was there the whole time, I would have slept soundly all night."

God is always watching us, but we don't believe in him enough to feel or see his support. When we get too caught up in our own problems we close ourselves off to the love of God, then wonder why we feel so alone.